Reigning cars and dogs

Top Dog, Dog Legs and Dog Ears were not man's best friend. But man, they were best friends.

One man in particular was not their best friend. You see, Eliza's dad was the proud owner of a classic sports car. The very one in fact that was now racing along the Californian coast, its shining red paint gleaming in the sun. The hugely expensive car that was being driven, rather rapidly, by his pet dog.

Eliza's dad would have probably enjoyed the drive, however his car never left the locked garage. Apart from on Saturdays when he carefully manoeuvred it the few yards on to the driveway for its weekly polish. Oh and today. When Top Dog smashed it through the locked garage door.

The sparkling silver bumper did a good job of breaking through the wooden barrier. Bits of wood bounced off the bonnet and over the heads of the three dogs sat in the open-top car. Eliza's dad watched in shock as his four-wheeled pride and joy disappeared down the drive leaving a trail of dust.

Firmly grasping the steering wheel with his grey paws, the Alaskan Husky stared ahead as he joined the winding road that hugged the Los Angeles beach. The dog driver occasionally glanced down at the dashboard where he had placed a picture of Eliza. The 9-year-old girl was the reason for this daring road trip.

They had been inseparable since Eliza took her first steps at his side when he was just a pup. It felt like only yesterday when she had clutched on to the grey fur on his back as she put one foot steadily in front of the other.

Her weight squashed him down and then she had suddenly yanked the ripples of skin on his back as she fell on to her bottom. But he didn't mind one bit. She grabbed his back and once more pulled herself up. Then Top Dog proudly watched as she let go and strolled away on her own across the living room. Her first steps and Top Dog had been there for this special moment.

Eliza's dad had brought Top Dog home the week after her mum had died. He needed to get away from their Santa Barbara home that had lost its heart, and had taken the 11-month-old Eliza to stay with his brother. Uncle Pete lived across the border in Canada and loved his Alaskan Malamutes.

'It's not like Marmite,' he had told his widowed brother. 'Everybody loves Malamutes. My Delores has just had four puppies. I need you to take one home and look after it. The company of a loving dog is just what you two need at this time.'

Eliza called him Dougie. It was one of the first words she had ever spoken – and it was on the day they had met. The girl's surprised dad exclaimed:

'Did you just say Dougie? What a perfect name! Yes we'll call him Dougie.'

Eliza's Uncle Pete was convinced she was trying to say doggie, but her father heard the name Dougie and it stuck (incidentally, later that same week when Pete bought a new pet budgie, Eliza's dad was certain she had suggested the name Bertie, though his brother was sure she was just labelling his new pet as a 'birdie').

Now Dougie wasn't top of the class. But the Alaskan Husky was a class act to the two lifelong friends he made soon after arriving at his new home. Which is why he was Top Dog to them – or indeed, Top Doug.

His next door neighbour Legs wasn't the fastest thing on four legs. But the big-hearted Bulldog would be at your side in a flash if you needed anything. And Ears' hearing was in no way in proportion to the size of the huge, brown-furred adornments that were currently flapping in the wind. In fact Ears' earmuffs should more accurately be named ear muffles as they did a great job in muffling any sounds. But the Cocker Spaniel, who lived on the local farm, would lend an ear whenever you needed to be heard.

And needing some doggy to listen to on that fateful August day, was Top Dog. So he called a meeting. It was a dog's breakfast. And I don't mean he made a mess of the meeting. But it was a meeting over breakfast for the trio of dogs. Sausages were eaten. Not hot dogs. Although the dogs eating the sausages were hot.

The sun beamed brightly on to the grass in the Santa Barbara garden. Beyond the fence, the sandy beach usually invited the dogs to head out for a morning play. But this summer's day was different and Top Dog had something to get off his soft, furry grey and white chest. His piercing brown eyes, which reflected the shimmering blue ocean in the distance, gazed at his two friends.

'I'm as sick as a dog', he announced. 'The vet told Eliza's father there's not much life left in the old dog.'

He went on: 'Every dog has its day they say, and today my friends is mine. For tomorrow the vet wants to send me to that great kennel in the sky.'

His friends sat staring in disbelief. Top Dog sensed the dismay at his rather unexpected news. Legs gulped, before his posh voice - imagine the Queen of Great Britain with a very deep voice - broke the silence:

'Please tell us this is just a shaggy dog story! This shouldn't happen to a dog... well not a dog like you.'

Now Bulldogs' faces always look a bit sad (or grumpy) but today this Bulldog managed to look sadder than ever.

'Do not be too down,' Top Dog said in a reassuring voice. 'In dogs' years, a day is surely like a whole week is to a human. And if it is my last day then I want to spend it with my two best buddies'.

Ears looked up and wiped away the tear drop that had appeared in one of his big brown eyes.

'You said you were *almost* ready to depart this life and head to doggy heaven?'

'Yes,' replied Top Dog. 'There is just one thing I need to do first...'

And this is where the adventure began, which became the three-dog night to remember...

2

Enemy held at Bay

'I just feel that as it's your last day, you should spend it with Eliza,' yapped Ears above the sound of the wind blowing his trademark appendages back as the car hurtled along the highway.

'She will be heartbroken if she never sees you again'.

'Trust me Ears,' replied Top Dog. 'I know it is best this way. I hate long goodbyes.'

'Where are we heading to Top Dog?' asked Legs. 'Do you have anywhere in mind?'

'I do. But first there are some things to tick off my bucket list.'

Before he could elaborate, the wailing sound of a police car siren halted their conversation. In the rear-view mirror, Top Dog could see the flashing red and blue lights of the chasing patrol car. Their old enemy Astrid the canine cop, the grumpiest Alsatian you could ever meet, was hanging out of the passenger door window.

She yelled at the joy-driving dogs in front to stop, as the equally stern looking policeman beside her closed in on the rear bumper of the red sports car.

'Fun's over. Stop the car now or I'll stop it for you', screamed Astrid.

'No way. You'll never take us alive!' Top Dog woofed over his shoulder.

The spokes of the classic car's wheels glistened in the sunlight as smoke poured out from the screeching tyres. Top Dog squeezed the accelerator pedal to the floor with his strong paw.

The car's red paintwork was a perfect match for the Golden Gate Bridge they were now speeding over. This made the damage to the car less noticeable when it hurtled into the metal frame of the bridge, just before they reached the other side. The car's paint which was scraped off was replaced with the similarly matched paintwork of the bridge.

Now Eliza's dad may not have noticed the dent this impact had made, and they might have just about got away with their joy ride, had it not been for the next impact. This was rather more noticeable as the car lost control and smashed through the barrier. It crashed nose first into the beach below.

The vehicle was now considerably shorter than when they had started the journey, and all three dogs felt lucky their lives had not been made considerably shorter as they prepared for their imminent death while flying through the air. Amazingly the soft beach cushioned their impact and they sat stunned in the wreckage of the once immaculate sports car.

They didn't have any time to waste as the police car skidded to a halt in the sand, causing a dusty cloud. As it cleared, they saw Astrid running towards them, her black tongue stuck out as her chubby cheeks flapped in the coastal breeze.

'Quick. To that balloon', shouted Top Dog.

Legs and Ears had not even noticed the blue hot air balloon that was further along the beach. They immediately bounded towards it and jumped into the basket. Top Dog cut the rope that was tying it down and they started to rise into the air.

Astrid leaped on to the side of the basket and held on with her yellow teeth. She growled so loudly, she could be heard above the roaring noise of the flame burner that Top Dog was frantically trying to turn up to full. As the flames soared and started to propel the balloon upwards ever faster, Astrid's eyes bulged as saliva poured from her slobby chops. The grizzly predator was unable to open her mouth to convey the rude words she wanted to pass on to the three fugitive dogs. Legs could see the stubborn dog would not let go.

'She's like a human with a phone [*translated from doggy language into "like a dog with a bone"*], when she wants to stop our fun', barked Legs, who certainly had a bone to pick with his gnarling nemesis.

'No doggy is going to stop my friend completing his mission today'.

A horrified Ears and Top Dog watched on as their short-legged pal launched himself over the edge of the basket. Ears peered over the side and was relieved to see his hero hound friend was still alive. Just a few feet below – the exact distance of Astrid's body with her outstretched tail to be precise – Legs' wide-opened eyes were staring back at him. And Astrid's tail was outstretched at this moment in time... with Legs' jaws locked firmly on to the end of it.

Astrid was not too pleased with this situation as you can imagine. Her own jaws tried desperately to remain locked on to the wicker side of the balloon. But she was already sliding down the basket as the balloon continued to ascend and the weight of the determined Bulldog below pulled her down.

As the balloon levelled with the top of the bridge, Legs plummeted to earth with Astrid's tail still in his mouth. And Top Dog was relieved to see Astrid was still attached to her tail as the airborne Alsatian assassin descended rapidly away from the balloon. Although needless to say, he was also rather concerned about the fate of his pal Legs. Astrid shared Top Dog's relief that her tail was still attached to her body, however she was more distracted by the fact that she was now flying through the air at high speed.

As Legs plummeted, he contemplated that he had not fully thought through his daring rescue plan. In those few seconds of free-fall he recalled Eliza's favourite book 'Some Dogs Do' and realised it was a bad time to discover this dog don't. Don't fly that is. As the two dogs plunged down to earth, Ears saw the shimmering green waves of the ocean below. It was then he remembered that this dog didn't swim either.

There were two splashes in quick succession as the pair belly flopped in to the sea. Ears watched as a tiny Astrid-shaped object doggy-paddled towards the beach below.

'Legs can't swim Top Dog!' he yelled and looked frantically for his friend in the water, but he was nowhere to be seen. 'We've got to save him'

'There's only one dog dying today and that's me' said a defiant Top Dog. 'Legs is not leaving us in a doggie bag today'.

Ears was thrown to the opposite side of the basket as Top Dog immediately set the balloon on its new course. Their craft was almost touching the water in seconds and Ears scanned the waves. Legs' doleful eyes met his friends and Ears leaned over the side and stretched out his large paw.

'You can do it Legs. Grab on!' yelled Ears.

Top Dog battled to manoeuvre the balloon as the bottom of the basket dipped into the water.

'Quick I can't hold this position much longer. We'll all sink' he barked.

A determined Legs grasped the bulldog's paw and, with a huge tug, yanked him in to the basket. His dripping wet body thudded to the floor just as the burners roared into life and they were once again climbing away from the coast. A dejected Astrid frowned on the beach as the blue vessel carrying her foes soared towards the clouds above the San Francisco Bay skyline.

'We did it!' a jubilant Top Dog announced as he continued with his piloting duties.

'Where are we heading to?' Ears asked.

'It's the place where I first met Eliza,' replied Top Dog, looking wistful. 'My birth home.'

'Ah right'' said Ears still none-the wiser, but not wishing to offend his friend with his ignorance.

He whispered to Legs who had now caught his breath back: 'Where did Eliza get Top Dog from?'

'Alaska,' came the reply.

'Don't be daft. No point waiting to ask her,' Ears said. 'We'll soon find out anyway when we arrive there!'

3

Dog's gone – a doggone day for dad

Eliza's dad surveyed the empty garage which had so hurriedly been vacated. He had been stood on the same spot just outside the entrance for some time now. The perplexed expression on his face had not changed since he witnessed what was surely the canine crime of the century. Eliza tapped her dad on the arm, with tears welling in her eyes, as she yelled up the driveway: 'Please come back'.

Her father was jolted back from his statue-like stupor and stuttered:

'W… w… we will get her back. I have every confidence in our local police force.'

'Her. You mean him?' Eliza replied, quite bemused.

'She is my precious four-wheeled treasure.' said her dad gravely.

'What about our precious four-legged treasure dad? He is far more important than some piece of metal!' wailed Eliza and burst into tears.

Her dad crouched down so his head was now level with hers. Putting a comforting arm around her, he softly spoke: 'Eliza. Let's go inside. We need to talk.'

Eliza had calmed down by the time she was sat at the breakfast bar in the kitchen, taking a sip of the orange juice her dad had just poured.

'Eliza,' he said, in the same solemn tone her teacher used when doing the class register each morning. 'About Dougie. You know he's not been himself recently. He's been very tired.'

'Yes I think he caught the cold from me,' said Eliza.

'No it's not a cold. I took him to the vet yesterday and well… well he's not very well at all. I was going to tell you today before all this happened.

'You see the vet said there is nothing she can do for Dougie I'm afraid. She can put him into a lovely sleep though and he won't suffer at all. I was going to let you say goodbye to him today but now he's disappeared.'

'No' said Eliza as tears formed in her large brown eyes. 'He can't be ill. The vet must be wrong.'

'I'm afraid not Eliza. And I think Dougie knew this himself. Which is probably why he's run away. Perhaps it is better this way'. Her dad said this with such conviction that he nearly convinced himself this was true, despite the barking mad car theft situation he found himself in.

'But I've not even had chance to say goodbye,' cried Eliza.

'Now you can remember him as he was Eliza, looking happy as he raced off down the drive'.

'And you can remember your silly car as it was. Looking all perfect and new as it raced up the drive with our garage door imprinted on its shiny bonnet!' yelled the eloquent Eliza. She took after her mum with her love of literature, which had given her a vocabulary way beyond her nine years.

'That's not fair Eliza,' retorted her dad. 'I loved Dougie as much as you did, ever since he came in to our lives. I'll miss him too honey'.

'All you care about is that car. First mummy left us and now Dougie. It's not fair', screamed Eliza and ran out of the room, knocking over the orange juice as she jumped down from her stool. The juice splashed over the gold photo frame on the kitchen table. Her dad looked at the picture, his eyes following a droplet as it slowly dribbled down the glass behind which a baby Eliza and her mummy were laughing back at him.

'Smile my two favourite girls' he had said that sunny day in the garden, as he pressed the button on top of the camera, inadvertently switching it off.

'It's the other button' his wife had yelled, and the pair were both laughing by the time he had switched it back on and located the correct switch to capture one of the happiest moments of his life.

The girls were staring back at him now in that photograph, the last one he had of them together. Only days later his wife had died suddenly. It turned out she had a brain haemorrhage. They had not had chance to say goodbye. He was determined this would not happen again. Eliza would get chance to say goodbye to Dougie. He grabbed the phone and dialled the police. It was only when the emergency operator spoke that he realised this would take a bit of explaining...

Meanwhile Eliza had run upstairs and flung herself on her bed, burying her sobbing face into her pink flowery duvet cover. After a few moments she sprang upright and wiped away the tears.

'What am I doing? I am being so selfish. Mummy would say I need to look after dad'.

Her Winnie the Pooh teddy bear – the one that had belonged to her mum that reminded Eliza of her most treasured book - looked back at her blankly, but she continued to talk to him anyway.

'Pooh, you once said to a friend "How lucky am I to have something that makes saying goodbye so hard".

'And this is so true. When mummy died, Daddy got me Dougie to look after me and be my best friend. And I am so lucky to have had him in my life all this time.

'But what has my Daddy got? He had his car to take his mind off things,' she explained maturely.

Eliza had grown up quickly after her mother died. She had to. After learning to walk, then talk, she quickly took up her role as the mother of the house. And with that came responsibilities. She often visited her mother's grave where she promised her mummy that she would look after her father. And today she realised she was not sticking to her vow to look after her Daddy.

'I know what to do Pooh,' she exclaimed. 'You stay here. I've got something I must do!'

She jumped down off her bed and emptied the large cardboard box that contained the scores of books she had amassed over the years. Grabbing the sticky tape and scissors from her bedside table she tossed them into the box along with her paints, and carried it downstairs. She paused at the bottom of the stairs to listen in on her dad's phone conversation:

'Can I describe the perpetrator? Well yes – he had grey hair and a red collar. '

There was a pause before he continued:

'No I didn't say he was wearing a red shirt. I said he was wearing a red collar. Dogs don't usually wear shirts… hello… hello… are you still there? I don't believe it. The emergency operator's hung up on me.'

Eliza heard the heavy tapping noise as her dad frantically redialled on his phone, but didn't eavesdrop any longer, and sneaked out to the garage. It was several hours before she re-emerged, feeling proud with what she had created inside. She wanted to show her dad and went to find him.

'Your tea's ready,' he said as she walked into the kitchen.

'I was just going to shout you. I'll grab something later. I've got a presentation to pull together for tomorrow so I'm going to crack on with that now.'

'But it's Sunday Daddy,' Eliza protested. 'And I've made something I wanted to show you.'

'I know treasure pie,' he replied. 'But it's really important. Can you show me later? How about tomorrow we go out for tea. I'm sure Dougie will turn up tomorrow. He'll probably come back with his tail between his legs and we can all walk down to the burger place on the beach.'

'OK Daddy,' Eliza said despondently. 'I'm tired so will probably have an early night after tea.'

'Yes good idea Eliza. Why don't you finish reading your latest book and get a good night's sleep. It's been a long day. I'll be in the study if you need me,' her dad said as he left the kitchen.

Eliza grabbed her plate from the table and threw herself down on Dougie's basket that was in the corner of the room. She ran her hand along the ruffled red blanket strewn with grey dog hairs. Dougie would always be sat there as Eliza tucked into her tea, so today the basket looked eerily empty. Eating in silence, Eliza saved a sausage on her plate for Dougie and placed it in the middle of the basket, before heading up to her bedroom.

4

Alaska here we come!

The blue balloon contrasted sharply with the snowy hills close below the basket. The eerie silence as the wicker vessel glided silently over the tops of the white-tipped fir trees was interrupted as the basket scraped one of the branches.

'Fire her up!' yelled a visibly nervous Ears to Top Dog. 'We're going to crash'.

'We're running out of power. We're going to have to land,' Top Dog growled back. 'Prepare yourselves for…'

Before he could finish his sentence, there was a crashing sound. The trio of dogs howled as they were vigorously thrown to one side of the basket, then the other in quick succession before they came to an abrupt stop. They found themselves in a heap on the floor, like a not so elegant animal trapeze act.

'Landing… I was going to say,' said Top Dog as he jumped down from the top of the shaggy dog pile carpet of the hot air balloon.

'Thanks for the warning,' said a furious Ears, who was next in the heap of hounds. Legs let out a whimper as Ears clambered off his squashed body.

'Hey. I've only just recovered from the soggy ordeal of my unexpected dip in the San Francisco bay.' he yelled.

'I know,' said Top Dog 'Hey Ears. Do you realise you were just sitting on the dog of the bay' and sang this to the tune of the 'Sitting on the Dock of the Bay' song.

Ears couldn't resist joining in: 'Ha-ha yes. Legs – it was just like that classic movie. You were the bird-dog of Alcatraz!'

'I'm glad you two think it's so amusing that I nearly drowned,' said Legs. 'That's twice I've almost died today. First I had to doggy paddle for my life, then I was nearly flattened by a pair of daft dogs. Now it looks like I'm going to freeze to death and become a slush puppy.'

'Hey Legs,' said Top Dog. 'As I said earlier, there's only one of us three musketeer mutts going to die today and that's me. Now let's enjoy this last adventure.'

'So which way are we heading?' asked Ears.

Top Dog pointed with his nose up the hill leading away from their icy crash landing site, through a tunnel of snow-capped fir trees. The trio trudged through the deep snow, their paws making footsteps several inches deep as they progressed slowly upwards.

5

Three-dog night

Eliza stared at the words written inside the front cover of her first edition Winnie the Pooh book as she lay on her bed. Her father had presented this to her on her 5th birthday, when she had started her lust for reading. The book had belonged to her mother since she was a girl. Her dad had inscribed a quote about dreaming, alongside the words 'Love Mummy x'.

While Eliza could not really remember her mother who had died before her first birthday, she nonetheless felt she knew her and often met her in her dreams. This inscription from her treasured book always gave her a warm feeling when she read it and made her feel her mother was always close by, living on in her heart. She jumped off her bed and walked across to the window, her tired eyes fixated on the full moon in the clear sky above.

'Dougie,' she said softly. 'Wherever you are tonight I hope you're warm and safe. Sleep tight.'

The bright moon beamed down on the mountainside, causing the crisp, freshly fallen snow to glisten as the three dogs huddled together to keep warm. Top Dog was sat in the middle, his teeth chattering together every now and then. Not because of the cold, as his canine comrades were doing a grand job acting as hairy heaters. No, the trio of trembling jaws was triggered by the occasional, ominous sounds that pierced the otherwise silent night.

The howling of a distant mountainside monster, or quite possibly a wolf, provided an intermittent and disconcerting soundtrack to the night-time stage of the dogs' expedition, and thwarted any attempts for Top Dog to fall asleep. Every time Top Dog's eyes closed for a few seconds, the noise would abruptly interrupt his peaceful thoughts and he was once again facing the moon above with his wide-eyed gaze.

'Do you know what the brightest star in the sky is called?' Top Dog suddenly spoke in a gruff voice that caused a synchronised shaking of his four-pawed radiators.

'I had just got to sleep!' yelled Ears.

'Wh… wh… where's the wolf gone?!' shouted a stunned Legs as he was snapped back to consciousness from his nightmare vision of a gnarling wolf trudging across the icy landscape, its hair covered in fluffy, wool-like snow… You could say he was dreaming of an actual wolf in sheep's clothing.

'It's Sirius,' Top Dog continued, ignoring his bemused chums. 'Otherwise known as the dog star. Don't you think it's fitting that the brightest and most important star should be named after the brightest and most important animal?'

'All I am thinking is that I hope that Great Bear in the sky is the only bear we see tonight as there are undoubtedly many great creatures prowling around these woods behind us,' responded Ears.

Top Dog looked across at the Ursa Major constellation of stars that was clearly visible in the black sky above.

'Eliza looked up at the stars through her telescope every night there was a clear sky, while I acted as her hot doggy water bottle to warm up her bed. I bet she's looking up tonight,' he said wistfully before his tone turned forlorn '… only her bed will be cold when she gets in tonight.'

'Well it won't be as cold as our frozen beds tonight,' said Legs. 'It's certainly a three-dog night tonight. My Australian cousin Digger told me about the Aboriginal saying 'a three-dog night'.

'Like here it gets cold overnight in the Australian Outback,' he continued as the other two dogs listened on intently.

'The Aborigines used to cuddle up to their dogs to keep warm. If it was really cold, they would need three dogs – hence it would be a three-dog night.'

'And Eliza's having her first ever no-dog night,' Top Dog sadly announced. 'I hope she's ok.'

'Hey Top Dog,' said Ears in a reassuring voice. 'We'll take good care of Eliza and keep your side of her bed warm whenever she needs us to.'

The three dogs fell silent as they huddled together, contemplating the significance of their moonlit discussion.

6

Dog dreams

Ears and Legs were soon snoring as Top Dog looked up at the full moon, becoming fixated by its incandescence. As he did so the Dog Star started to flicker, before moving slowly towards it, leaving a flaming trail in the sky. He watched intrigued by this unexpected cosmic display, until Sirius collided with the moon. There was a fantastic flash of light that briefly illuminated the mountainside, before all fell into darkness again.

The moon now appeared to be much closer and Top Dog squinted at the shining sphere, where between two large craters he could see something moving on the dust-like surface. As his eyes remained transfixed, he found himself floating up towards the moon, rapidly flying through the cool night air as he zoomed towards the object that was now skipping along the moon. His paws gently touched down and he felt the moon's rocky surface. Before he had chance to survey his landing site, he felt a pair of warm arms around his neck.

'Dougie!' exclaimed the familiar voice. 'I've missed you so much. I've found this stick for you to fetch'.

Top Dog turned around and watched as Eliza heaved at the United States of America flag embedded in the moon's surface. A cloud of moon dust flew up as the flag was tugged out of the ground and Top Dog watched as Eliza flung it into the distance. It flew through the air and Top Dog immediately started chasing after it, with Eliza running by his side, laughing loudly as they cantered along. Top Dog pounced on to the wooden stick, his paws scraping up moon dust as they slid along the surface.

In the far distance beyond, he could see what looked like a magnificent marble, coloured green and blue. 'What on earth was it?' he briefly wondered, before he realised that Earth, it was.

He obediently returned the stick to Eliza whose face was beaming. It was an equally marvellous sight for Top Dog. The happy hound jubilantly leapt into the air, but unlike on Earth, instead of landing back on his paws he found himself slowly ascending. Floating away from Eliza's smiling face he felt free. He watched as the moon became smaller and smaller as he rose higher and higher in to the blackness of space. All became silent and peaceful. A bright light above caused him to look up. He was suddenly accelerating towards the brightest star. Faster and faster he found himself spiralling upwards, until the vivid whiteness swallowed the blackness in a fantastic flash.

Eliza opened her eyes as her dark bedroom was suddenly thrown in to brightness.

'You've slept in Eliza. Come on get up!' her dad was saying as he drew back the curtains, causing the sun to stream into her dark bedroom.

Eliza was smiling as she was jolted out of her sleep and sat up stunned.

'I was just with Dougie,' she exclaimed. 'It felt so real. We were playing on the moon.'

'Aww that's nice Eliza,' said her dad, not really listening as he picked up some clothes strewn on the floor. 'Breakfast's on the table. Get dressed quickly. I need to be in work early today.'

Eliza threw back her quilt and looked at the grey dust on her hands and in her bed.

'Moon dust!' she said.

'How have you managed to get so much sand in your bed Eliza?' asked her dad as he headed out of the door.

'Get yourself showered quickly!'

Eliza smiled as she blew the dust off her hands and jumped out of bed.

Meanwhile Top Dog opened his eyes abruptly. The bright white of the Dog Star in his dream was replaced with a vision of equally bright whiteness. He squinted as he surveyed the snow-covered landscape, illuminated by the morning sun rising above the trees on the horizon.

'You're back with us,' said the familiar voice of Ears. 'You must have been having an exciting dream from all the noisy yelps you were making.'

'I was with Eliza in space,' Top Dog responded. 'Then I flew up to the Dog Star.'

'You cannot be Sirius,' wise-cracked Legs.

'I am being serious,' retorted the astronautic canine dreamer. 'I had one last play with Eliza and it really was out of this world.'

'Well back in the real world we've got some walking to do if we want to reach our destination before the sun goes down,' said Legs.

'Indeed,' replied Top Dog, now feeling like he had been brought back down to Earth with a bump. 'I feel it's now time to fill you both in on the whole reason for this trip. You will have a very special package to deliver.'

His two companions looked at each other puzzled, and Ears was first to speak up: 'As you know, I'm all ears. What special package?'

'We're heading to meet my dear big brother Oscar. I've not seen him since last Christmas when Eliza took me with her to visit her uncle at my birth home. Oscar's just become a father of four pups – three daughters and my nephew, Buster. Oscar says he is the spitting image of me all those years ago when Eliza came to take me home with her. Now as that old human phrase goes, it's a case of out with the old – me… and in with the nephew.'

'I think the phrase is actually 'in with the new'', interjected Legs. 'And you're not that old, Top Dog!'

'I'm old enough and as you know you can't teach an old dog new tricks,' Top Dog replied. 'But you can teach a new dog some old tricks of the trade. And that's what I intend to do with Buster. I don't have long, but I want to make sure Buster is ready to step up to being the best companion and loyal servant he can be for Eliza.'

'And so you want us to take him back to Eliza and take your place?' asked Legs. 'They're big boots to fill. Your paws have left a huge imprint in Eliza's life.'

'You're very kind Legs,' sighed Top Dog. 'But alas, my time is done and it's time to hand over the baton to the next generation. Under your guidance, I know Buster is up to the job. Oscar reassures me he is already showing he is destined for great things. And there's no greater thing than being a pooch partner for Eliza. There's an old family mantra my great grandma passed on to me as she took her last breath. It's called "Unleash The Do-Gooding Dog Within" and it goes like this:

"Do-gooding, the word has a proud dog within,

No-gooding has no dog, it's a canine sin.

So grow proud, and oodles of do-gooding do,

No dawdling now, just unleash the top dog in you."'

'Wow. What did your great gran die of – a twisted tongue?' wise-cracked Legs. 'Sorry only kidding. Buster sounds just like you - a right goody two-shoes. Or should I say a good-doggy four-paws. And I mean that in the nicest possible way Tops.'

'I've always thought you have a very apt name Doug,' said Ears.

'It's never been about me. You certainly put the U in Dog. You've always put Eliza first.'

'All I've ever wanted is to do good for you Eliza,' sighed Top Dog, looking up to the moon that was still visible, just starting to fade away in the early morning sky now the sun was rising.

'Let's proceed. We'll be there in a few hours.'

7

Astrid strike

The crunching of paws, leaving imprints several inches deep in the freshly fallen snow, was the only sound to be heard as the trio trudged on.

Edging towards their final destination, Top Dog was striding ahead in his self-elected role as leader of the pack – his ancestral skills as a sled dog made him the natural leader for this Arctic expedition, despite the fact that most of his nine years had been in a sunny Californian climate. Nevertheless, he now felt in his element and more determined than ever to reach his goal.

As they approached the summit of a snow-covered hill, a distant humming sound caused the dogged travellers to abruptly stop. Ears cocked his head to the side as the humming sound increased in intensity, until it became a roaring cacophony at odds with the serene, tranquil surroundings that had been their backdrop for the past several hours.

Expressions of confusion quickly transformed into wide-eyed shock in a moment of perfect synchronisation across the trio's faces, as a Spitfire warplane suddenly appeared over the brow of the hill. It flew towards the bewildered dogs who were rooted to the spot in terror.

The plane was so low they could clearly see the pilot's face as they were forced to suddenly dive for cover face first into the icy hillside. A large net was flung out of the plane and Astrid's manic glare was fixed on them as the dogs momentarily disappeared under a cloud of dispersed powdery snow.

As the three dogs scrambled back to their feet, they were relieved to see the net had missed the target and its green ropes lay on the snow. Their relief was short-lived as they were horrified to see the plane making a sharp bank to the left as it turned back round to face them again. There was an ear-splitting noise that echoed through the hills as the old machine's engine clattered into life and thrusted towards them.

The three dogs were running as fast as they could manage through the deep snow which felt like wading through treacle – which Top Dog mused was a very apt analogy as they were facing a sticky end on the mountainside.

Suddenly, they were given an increased urge to accelerate through the snow as the sound of rapid machine-gun fire drowned out even the roar of the engine. The three were running for their lives as thick green netting, rather than bullets, was fired into the snow just inches from their paws, as they now glided not so gracefully over the icy surface. Top Dog could feel the whoosh of the plane's rotor fanning the cold air on to his tail it was now that close. He cowered down as the plane thundered over his head.

Yelps of despair could be heard as the noise of the Spitfire reduced from the deafening din to a more distant murmur again as the plane's nose lifted up into the air. Top Dog was horrified to see that while he had ducked down, Legs had slipped over the ice that sloped down towards the cliff face just ahead of them. He watched as Legs disappeared over the edge. Ears was just behind him and Top Dog could see he had managed to stop himself facing the same fate as Legs, and was bent over the cliff edge. Top Dog ran towards him and peered over. There was a sheer drop that led down to a canyon, a huge distance beneath them. He could see Ears' right paw was outstretched. Grasping on to it was Legs, whose eyes were wide open in fear.

'Quick Top Dog. He's pulling me towards him! Hold on to me and heave!' yelled Ears.

Top Dog sprang into action and grabbed his friend, trying not to be distracted by the war plane that was now banking round in the distance ahead of them. Ears and Top Dog pulled as hard as they could while struggling to grip in the icy snow.

Exhausted and now panting heavily, they gave one last desperate attempt to tug Legs back on to the top of the cliff, but Ears felt his friend's paw slipping away. In horror he watched as Legs lost his grip and disappeared out of view as he and Top Dog collapsed backwards on to the cliff top.

Before they had time to comprehend what had happened, Ears and Top Dog heard the roar of the plane once more increasing in intensity. The pair glanced up to see the Spitfire heading towards them, this time much lower than before. It was heading straight towards them and there was nowhere to hide – and no time to move. They cowered down and waited for the plane to crash into them.

Suddenly they heard the aircraft fly over the top of them. Top Dog peered anxiously through his paws to see it had changed direction at the last minute and was veering over the cliff at a 90-degree angle with its left wing pointing up to the sky. Rapidly losing altitude, it started plummeting to the depths of the canyon.

Ears jumped up and the pair peered over the cliff to see the plane explode in a ball of flames as thick black smoke rose towards them. Then a red parachute opened up some distance below, above the plumes of smoke. But they were distracted from this sight by a rustling in the snow just behind them. They were surprised to see Legs staring back at them.

'We thought you were… were… a goner,' stammered Top Dog.

'So did I. For the third time today,' said Legs. 'I'm beginning to think I was meant to be a cat with all these lives I seem to have!'

'But how…?' said Ears.

'When you hopeless hounds literally lost grip of the situation and failed to hang on to me, I fell onto a branch jutting out of the cliff face. I managed to cling on and somehow clamber back to the top,' Legs calmly recollected.

'When I arrived back at the summit I had a boomerang-shaped twig from the branch in my jaws. In that instant as I stared at Astrid's ugly mug glaring through the cockpit window, I thought of my cousin Digger in Australia. I remembered how he told me the boomerang was used as a hunting weapon by the Aborigines.

'In that moment as Astrid drew closer I realised I had one chance. I seized my opportunity as she pointed the plane towards you two cowering in the snow just in front of me. Then I flung my makeshift boomerang at the window and it cracked the screen right between her manic eyes. This caused her to crash over the cliff.'

Top Dog and Ears just lay there, no longer having the energy to speak, but in total awe at their friend. It was several moments before Top Dog got his breath back: 'Well I bet that Spitfire has seen many dogfights in its time, but this was one dog fight too many. And we won.'

'And never mind Spitfire,' said Legs. 'I want to fire my spit on to Astrid's grave down there.'

'Erm,' said Ears. 'It might be a little hasty for that. We saw Astrid parachute to safety. So I don't think we've seen the last of her just yet.'

'But we certainly won't be seeing her in a hurry,' said Top Dog.

'It will take her a week to climb back up that mountain. Let's catch our breaths here and eat some lunch before our last trek to Oscar's pad. We'll soon be there now. It's not far.'

8

A car bonny copy for dad

Eliza slurped up the last remnants of the chocolate milkshake as she watched the waves crash on to the beach outside. Her dad had amazingly kept his promise to take her to their local seaside burger bar after school, and was only five minutes late picking her up.

She had been disappointed when Dougie was not in his usual place, hanging out of the back window of her father's car to greet her when she walked out of the school gates.

'Well I'm dying to know what big secret you have waiting for me in the garage,' her dad said as they headed out to the car park after finishing off his cheese burger.

Eliza just smiled and they didn't speak on the 5-mile drive home along the coastal highway, both listening to a song by her dad's favourite band from the UK, James.

Her parents had met at a James gig in New York, where her dad was on a business trip and her mother was on her first vacation to the USA, accompanied by her best friend. The group was from her mum's home city in Manchester and as the opening chords of their anthemic single Sit Down played out, she had sat down alongside the man stood to her left. Straight away they realised they were the only ones in the concert hall who had done this (fans used to do this at the band's earlier gigs, but twenty years on and it was maybe less cool to do this now). However, like two fat polar bears that Top Dog may encounter in his Alaskan adventure, it was a great ice breaker and the initially embarrassed pair remained with their bottoms planted on the hard floor of the auditorium. Completely oblivious to the frantic fans energetically jumping up and down to the song, the couple were instantly engrossed in each other's conversation as they sat down in their own cocoon – and they were inseparable from that moment.

The next song to play on the car stereo was not one Eliza had heard before, and the lyrics of the chorus mentioned the moon, making her think of the vivid dream from last night.

As she heard the words, she glanced back to the empty seats behind. For a moment she imagined a perfect parallel universe where she was sat alongside Dougie in the back, and pictured her mum in the passenger seat where she was currently sitting. Her father's voice jolted her back to reality.

'Here we are,' he said as he parked up their driveway.

Eliza jumped out and ran to the battered garage door, still bearing the signs of its impact with the classic convertible.

'Well Daddy,' she started. 'Close your eyes and I'll bring my surprise out. I hope you like it.'

Her father obligingly shut his eyes behind his designer aviator sunglasses, where the mirrored lenses reflected the light blue chequered pattern of Eliza's school uniform before she disappeared into the garage. She re-emerged a few moments later, scraping her large cardboard creation along the sandy stoned driveway, where a family of ants scurried out of the way and vanished between the cracked paving.

'OK dad. You can open your eyes,' she announced.

Her dad squinted as the sun hit his eyes and then peered down at the freshly painted red piece of artwork that confronted him. He was amazed at the sight before him. It was a genuine, slightly scaled down, replica version of his stolen car, albeit lovingly carved out of cardboard boxes by his daughter. He stood staring in awe at the level of detail, from the wipers attached to the makeshift cling film windscreen, to the accurately rendered licence plate.

Walking round the creation, he soon realised the attention to detail extended to the interior, where he could see the dashboard with amazingly crafted dials made out of old yoghurt cartons and even a gearstick created from a garlic baguette. Tears streamed down his face and he was unable to stop the uncontrollable sobbing that followed.

'Don't you like it Daddy?' asked Eliza, taken aback by his unexpected display of emotion.

'No Eliza. It's nothing like my car,' he stuttered.

'It was only meant to cheer you up until you got your actual car back,' said Eliza.

'I mean there's no comparison,' continued her father. 'What I'm trying to say is I wouldn't swap what you've made for me here with my real car. I love this.

'Oh Eliza,' he said as he pulled out a handkerchief to wipe his eyes. 'I've been neglecting you and I'm so sorry. Your mum would be immensely proud of you.'

In reality, there were flaws in the design of Eliza's first attempt at manufacturing an automobile. She needn't have been concerned about being issued a writ by the original car's manufacturer for infringing the trademarked design. But Eliza's dad didn't care. His proud parent eyes could only see perfection in the work of his daughter.

'I don't even want my car back now,' he said. 'There's only room in the garage for one and yours is far more precious to me.'

He hugged his daughter and kissed her on top of her head, and Eliza felt like she never wanted him to let go. However, the ringing of a phone caused him to release his grasp of her.

'It's my boss,' he said, looking at the screen of his mobile phone. 'I ought to answer it Eliza.'

He then lifted the phone up towards his ear, but instead of answering it, he flung his arm back and proceeded to toss the gadget high in the air up the driveway, as if he was chucking a stick for Dougie to fetch. His own dog had done a better job of being a father figure to Eliza. But from now on he vowed to always put her first. He grabbed back hold of Eliza and held her tight. Eliza's dad knew things were going to be different from this day.

9

Dying to meet you

'I have certainly had a dog's life my friends,' sighed Top Dog as he collapsed into the snow, where crunchy icicles clung to his hairy chin.

'But I feel my time has come, for I am dog-tired.'

'But we're so close now,' said Legs. 'We can't give in now.'

Top Dog's eye lids slowly closed and, using up what felt like the last breaths of his energy, muttered in a croaky voice:

'You two must complete the mission without me. Now it's time to let this sleeping dog lie.'

The exhausted hound briefly smiled as a picture of Eliza's smiling face appeared in a hallucinatory moment, before all turned to darkness for Top Dog.

'Wake up!' yelled Ears, yanking Top Dog's slobbering jowls from each side of his face to expose the yellow tinted teeth below.

The loose flaps of skin pinged back with great velocity, shaking the Alaskan Malamute's head from side to side. Still Top Dog remained in a comatose state. Heaving his limp body backwards, Legs and Ears dropped him down on to the wooden base they had hastily assembled in the last half an hour since Top Dog had passed out (not passed away they were relieved to find). Top Dog landed with a thud on the hard rectangular base, created from several broken branches. He opened one eye and looked a little perturbed.

'Is this the base of a coffin you have started building? There's no need. This snowy floor can be my grave. Just bury me under this white carpet.'

'It's not a coffin. It's a sleigh. We need a crash course in being husky sled dogs. Are you up to it Top Dog?' asked Ears.

'It would be very much a crash course,' replied Top Dog. 'I've never so much as seen a sleigh before. Never mind pulled one across a treacherous mountainside!'

'Well it will be a case of the blind dogs leading the blind dogs then,' said Legs. 'We intend to use this to transport you to your brother's home. We're not giving up now.'

'Please just let me die here in peace rather than die in pieces in a horrific sled crash on this mountainside!' Top Dog said in his sternest voice as he tried to shout, but couldn't quite muster up the strength in his weary state.

'We went back and found those nets Astrid threw at us from her warplane. She really helped us out there providing us with them ropes,' said Ears.

'Hold on tight,' he continued as Top Dog saw his friends had made reigns harnessed round their backs from the green strands of netting which were strapped to the sleigh. 'We're off!'

Top Dog was flung backwards as the sledge shot forwards and started a sharp descent towards the valley below. The trio were soon hurtling down the mountainside and Top Dog found the icy cold wind was highly effective in bringing him back to full consciousness. He started to wish he was asleep and this was some horrible dream as the sledge swerved violently between towering trees.

Ears glanced back towards him: 'Isn't this fun?!'

Top Dog closed his eyes and didn't dare open them again as he desperately clung on to the wooden frame of what he thought must be his open-top hearse, waiting for the crunching impact of one of the trees that he could sense whizzing past at breakneck speed. The crunch never came though. Instead, Top Dog felt his nightmare taxi come to a gradual halt as they reached the bottom of the slope. He peered ahead and suddenly found he had a new-found spurt of energy, generated by the sight that greeted him.

'Oscar!' yelled Top Dog as he saw his brother bounding towards him. 'I've been dying to meet you.'

'I'm pleased to see you again too dear brother,' replied Oscar as he darted out of the wooden cabin and up the snow-covered path, at the home he shared with Eliza's Uncle Pete.

'No, Oscar. I really am dying,' said Top Dog solemnly, as the pair hugged each other.

'Snap,' said Oscar.

Each took a step back, and the pair stood peering at each other. To Legs and Ears, there could have been a mirror in the icy wilderness as it looked like two doppelgangers taking part in a staring competition. The dogs could have been identical twins, although Top Dog was two years younger than his Alaskan sibling.

'You better come inside and warm up. You look like you've had a tough journey here,' said Oscar.

'You could say that,' responded Top Dog.

'Well come in and I'll make you some supper while we catch up. I think there may be a bit to do,' said Oscar, leading the trio of visitors inside.

The pan sizzled as the three intrepid travellers watched on expectantly, their mouths drooling as the pancake cooked. Oscar expertly tossed it in the air and it returned to the hot bubbling oil with a satisfactory splattering sound.

'Brilliant flipping,' congratulated Legs.

'Flipping brilliant,' cheered Ears.

'Thanks,' said the proud canine chef. 'I think Dougie is most in need of some food.'

Oscar then poured on some maple syrup and a sprinkling of beefy biscuits before rolling up the ingredients in his freshly prepared golden envelope. Top Dog devoured it in a single gulp and licked his lips as Oscar started preparing the next pancake.

'What did you mean when you said snap?' inquired Top Dog.

Oscar calmly responded without diverting his eyes from the culinary task he was engaged with.

'Well I have an incurable disease brother. I have only days to live like you.'

'But is there nothing Eliza's Uncle Pete can do?' said Top Dog abruptly.

'No. But I know my time has come and I've accepted it,' replied Oscar in a matter-of-fact tone, throwing the second pancake into the air as he spoke.

'But he's a vet! Surely…'

'No,' interrupted Oscar. 'That's why he knows there's nothing that can be done. I'm only sad that I have had two more years on this beautiful earth than you. It is just not fair dear brother.'

Top Dog was now looking into his brother's eyes, as his gaze had been averted from the frying pan.

'I heard of your predicament Dougie,' said Oscar. 'Pete and Eliza's dad were Skyping about your diagnosis as I lay in front of the log fire the other night. Eliza's dad was most concerned about breaking the news to Eliza.'

'Which is why I'm here,' said Top Dog. 'Your son, my nephew, needs a new home. And he can take my place. Legs and

Ears are here to ensure Buster's safe journey to his new home. You couldn't hope for a better home for him Oscar.'

Oscar embraced his brother.

'We can both go to our graves with the knowledge that the ones we love most are in safe hands,' Top Dog whispered into his brother's ear, staring towards his best pals Ears and Legs, who watched on with tears in their eyes.

10

In doggy heaven

'They're both happy in doggy heaven,' said Eliza as she walked up the field behind her Uncle Pete's home with Buster at her side.

Three weeks had passed since Buster turned up on her doorstep. Her dad was a little flabbergasted to say the least, but welcomed the mini version of Dougie into their home. Around Buster's collar was a message, scrawled on rather dog-eared paper it has to be said, that simply read: 'Knick-knack paddy whack, give this dog a home, Top Dog's soul's come rolling home.'

On seeing Eliza's jubilant reaction to the sight on their doorstep following a week of anguish at losing Dougie, her father had accepted the admittedly unusual and unexpected delivery that day without questioning it. And Buster made himself at home, immediately acquainting himself with his uncle's abode and taking his spot on Eliza's bed.

Her dad decided it would be good for them to visit his brother in Alaska to have a break from the recent traumatic events, and as soon as they arrived, Eliza wanted to see Dougie's final resting place. Her Uncle Pete led her out of his back door, across the wooden terrace and out on to the field where Buster's small legs disappeared into the crunchy snow with each footstep as he bounded out in front. At the far end of the field they stopped as they arrived at a wooden cross sticking out of the ground, where a patch of snow had been cleared to mark out the grave.

'I dug a hole here for the two dogs,' Uncle Pete broke the silence. 'I'm getting a proper gravestone made… but it will only have Oscar's name on it Eliza.'

Before she could respond, she turned to see her dad walking over the horizon. The early morning sun glaring behind him caused her to screw up her eyes. As she squinted in the bright light, she saw a familiar silhouette of an animal strolling by his side. As their eyes met, the dog started leaping towards her, jumping over the snow with each stride.

'Dougie?' she stuttered. 'My Top Dog? But…'

'It's Dougie,' announced her uncle as Eliza caught Top Dog mid-flight as her excited, panting pet dived into her arms, causing the pair to plunge in to the snow. Eliza was laughing and crying at the same time as Dougie yelped and licked her face.

'I realised I could save Dougie,' said her uncle. 'It was all thanks to Oscar. You see, Dougie needed a new liver. And his dying brother was the perfect donor. It's pretty rare for a dog to have a transplant, but I knew I could do it. He's been convalescing for the past fortnight since the operation, but he's been gaining strength by the day.'

'I think it was meant to be Eliza,' said her dad as he approached Oscar's grave. 'Pete couldn't save Oscar, but he can live on through Dougie.'

As his daughter smiled up at him, he saw his wife smiling back at him and realised that she too lived on, through their own special daughter.

Top Dog looked up at Eliza and in the sky above, the moon was still visible as the sun was rising. Observing the reflection of the moon in her best friend's eyes, Eliza turned to glance up at it. Just beyond she observed a bright star. The pair stared silently up at it as Eliza cuddled Dougie, now laid on his back with his white chest in the air, enjoying being tickled by her.

Her dad smiled proudly and said: 'It's certainly a dog's life.'

Printed in Great Britain
by Amazon